For my mother (my queen)
and my Uncle Darryl (my guardian angel).

www.mascotbooks.com

LISTEN UP, BUTTERCUP!

©2021 Kiera Ezell. All Rights Reserved. No part of this publication may be reproduced, stored in a retrieval system or transmitted in any form by any means electronic, mechanical, or photocopying, recording or otherwise without the permission of the author.

For more information, please contact:
Mascot Books
620 Herndon Parkway #320
Herndon, VA 20170
info@mascotbooks.com

Library of Congress Control Number: 2021904434

CPSIA Code: PRT0321A
ISBN-13: 978-1-64543-856-4

Printed in the United States

Ebba is a big black bear with a big heart. She is as gentle as a butterfly. Even though many forest animals fear her, she is a joy to be around. Ebba enjoys her daily walks in the forest with her best pal, Daisy the squirrel. Daisy is a tiny squirrel with a big mouth that gets her in big trouble.

"Ebba, what shall we have for lunch today?" asked Daisy. "I was thinking green bugs casserole with a side of berry and fish slaw."

"I have not thought about lunch yet," replied Ebba.

"Well, for a snack, maybe we could visit Ranger Granger and scoop up some of that delicious trail mix that he keeps for the bears," Daisy said, rubbing her belly. "I don't want to go there, Daisy," Ebba shook her head. "The last time I saw Ranger Granger, my life was in danger."

"He wants you in that zoo, Buttercup!" yelled Daisy. "I wonder if he would let me visit you there?"

"Knock it off, Daisy!" replied Ebba softly.

"LISTEN UP, BUTTERCUP!"

screamed Daisy. "We have to come up with an incredibly well-thought-out plan!"
"I'm not good at thinking, Daisy," said Ebba.
"Remember, that is why I have you as a friend," she said with a smile.
"Oh yeah, I am the smart one," grinned Daisy. "Well, come on. We will worry about those troubles later."
"What does that mean?" asked Ebba.
"Troubles?" said Daisy. "Oh! Nothing . . . let's go!"

The two went off into the deep forest. They stumbled upon Max the beaver. He was a meanie beanie, but he was very petrified of Ebba.

Max was extremely lazy. He once told the other animals that he only exercised by lifting his delicious wooden log snacks.

"Max! Max! What's that?" Daisy asked. "Wow!" she exclaimed, pointing at his belly.

"DO NOT START THAT TODAY!" he yelled.

"Ha! Ha! May I start tomorrow?" asked Daisy.

Max then started to wobble toward Daisy, but when he saw Ebba appear from behind the stump, he scampered away into his hole.

The two traveled down the path, and they noticed Victoria, the sassy fox, singing to a little, gray rabbit. Poor rabbit. Victoria would sing to her prey before she would attack them. Ebba knew not to bother Victoria, but Daisy threw small pebbles at the rabbit. This made Victoria furious, and she stopped singing instantly.

"I guess you will be my lunch now!"
Victoria exclaimed while rolling her eyes at Daisy.

"Yep, eat Ebba first. I'll be your dessert," laughed Daisy.

"EBBA? Where is she? I didn't see her," Victoria asked.

"Hi Vic—" Ebba started.

But before Ebba could greet her, Victoria dashed into the woods as fast as lightning. Daisy enjoyed being a pest to the other animals. She would bother them and go on as if nothing had happened.

Ebba walked toward a hole that Daisy was looking into.

"Daisy!" Ebba yelled. "What are you doing over there?"

But Daisy continued to look down into the hole.

Ebba walked closer and poked Daisy on the top of her head. Daisy's hind legs jumped into the air. When she finally landed on her feet, she poked Ebba's face.

"WOULD YOU LIKE FOR ME TO POKE YOU? NOW, SIT THERE AND LISTEN,"

Daisy said.

Ebba sat on the edge of the water bank.

"Over there is an enormous hole . . . are you listening?" she yelled at Ebba.

"Yes, Daisy, but what does that hole have to do with us?"
"If you would listen up, I could tell you. Now focus, Buttercup." Daisy came closer to Ebba and started to whisper, "Ebba, Ranger Granger is trapped inside that hole. I think we should cover it up with dirt and water. That way, he won't be able to capture you and put you in the zoo."

"Uhhh. Daisy, I don't think that . . ." Ebba started, but Daisy darted right for Ebba's head again.
"Listen up, Buttercup . . . you walk around every day in fear of being put away in a zoo. You are always sad and moping around. You could put him away!" Daisy yelled.

Ebba slowly walked over to the hole. Ranger Granger was in distress and covered in sweat. When he glanced up, he recognized Ebba. Instead of asking for help, he started to yell.

"Oh! You just wait . . . I'll get you as soon as I get out from here!"

This startled Ebba. She stepped slowly away from the hole, causing her to bump into Daisy.

"You see, I told you to get rid of him," Daisy said.

"That's not a nice thing to do," Ebba replied as she shook her head.

As the two were discussing whether or not to help Ranger Granger, a mean rattlesnake began to slither down into the hole.

"Look! Look!" screamed Daisy. "Looks like we can rest now. That rascal will take care of Mr. Granger for you, Ebba."
Ebba did not move. She did not want to get rid of Ranger Granger, nor did she want him to be harmed by the snake. She walked back toward the hole. She could see the snake getting closer to Ranger Granger.
"Daisy, we have to get him out. We just have to," said Ebba.

"Listen up, Buttercup! He wants you out of here. Have you forgotten that?" said Daisy.

Looking down at her reflection in the water, Ebba began to think about all the times she gave up on herself and had not believed in herself. She wanted to be stronger. Not just in size, but in heart.

"HELLO, BUTTERCUP?" yelled Daisy.

"Yes," Ebba replied. "But Daisy, just because someone does things to harm you does not mean you should do the same to them."

For the first time in her life, Ebba decided to think of a plan.

"Daisy, we are going to get him out. First, we will have Max and Victoria assist us. Max is great at building things. We can have him build a ladder to throw down in the hole. Then, we will have Victoria distract the snake with her sassy singing. Lastly, I will need you to encourage me the entire time so I don't get afraid of Ranger Granger."

"Okay, but do you think they will listen to you?" asked Daisy.

"Yes, I know they will," replied Ebba, even though she wasn't sure herself.

Ebba walked over to the hole to check on Ranger Granger. He was curled up in a tight knot. The snake was hissing as he continued down the hole. Ebba turned around and immediately darted toward the woods to find Max and Victoria.

Daisy followed Ebba running wildly and yelling, **"Buttercup, slow down!"**

Ebba ignored Daisy's remark. Demanding Max and Victoria to assist her was going to be a big task, and . . . oh boy, was she nervous!

When they finally made it to the stump, they found Max and Victoria sunbathing and chatting. They were discussing whether squirrels and chipmunks were the same, but when they caught a glimpse of Ebba running in their direction, they both jumped to their feet.

Daisy felt she had to be the first one to speak so they would assist Ebba.
"Listen . . . I have some important . . . " Daisy started.
"Oh! Why don't you run off!" yelled Max.
"Why don't you lay off the bark jerky, hot breath?" replied Daisy.

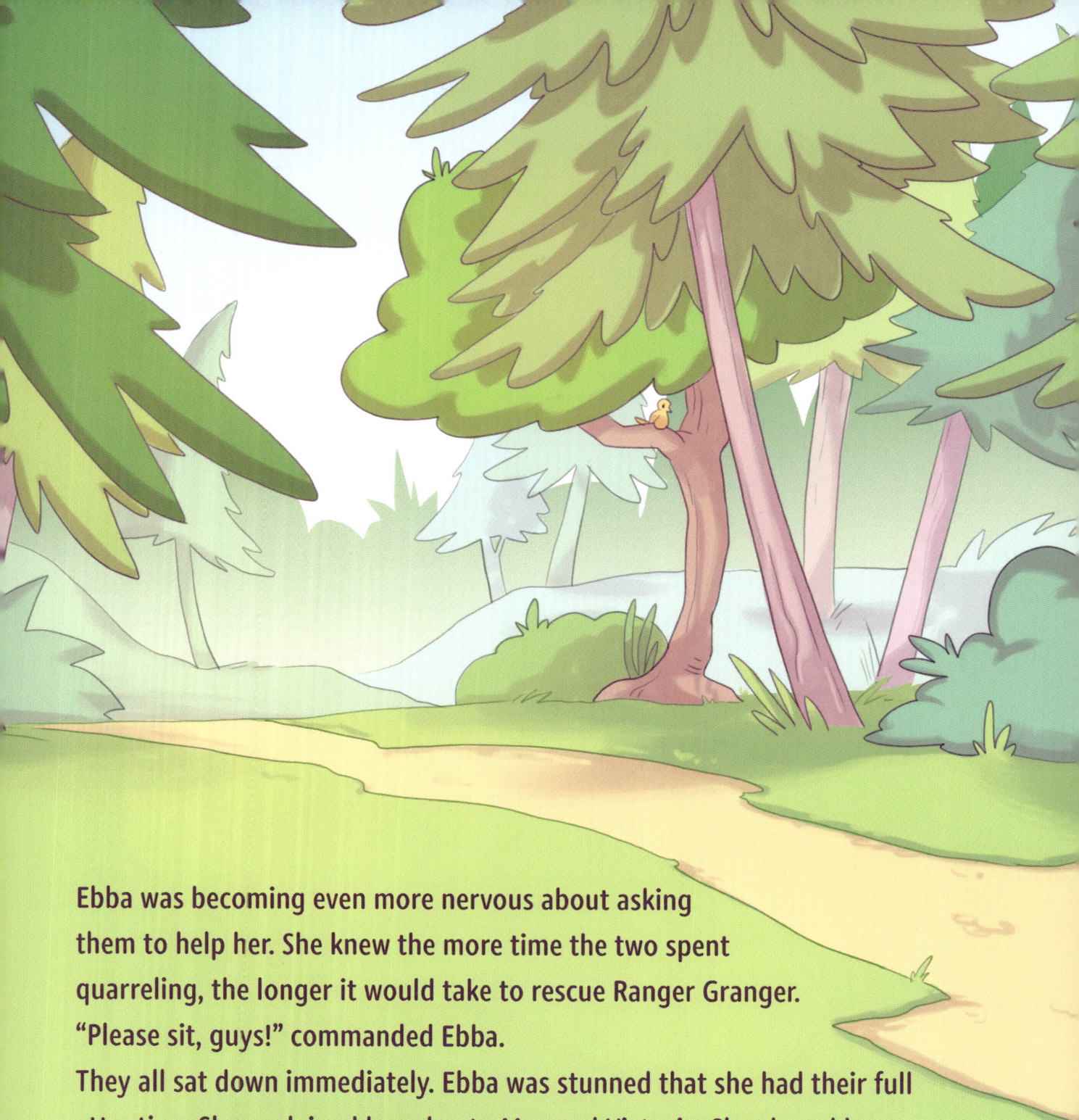

Ebba was becoming even more nervous about asking them to help her. She knew the more time the two spent quarreling, the longer it would take to rescue Ranger Granger. "Please sit, guys!" commanded Ebba.
They all sat down immediately. Ebba was stunned that she had their full attention. She explained her plan to Max and Victoria. She shared how everyone would contribute to getting Ranger Granger out of the hole. Max informed Ebba that the only way he would help would be if Daisy left him alone. Daisy agreed hesitantly.

The four animals rushed back to the hole to help rescue Ranger Granger. He was screaming from the top of his lungs when they approached the hole because the snake was very close. Max had a ladder that was already built, so Ebba took it and threw it down to Ranger Granger. Ebba instructed Victoria to start with her singing.

"Oh, Christmas tree! Oh, Christmas tree!"
Victoria sang.
"WHAT? Are we saving Santa Claus or Mr. Granger here?" asked Daisy.

Despite the fact that it was a Christmas carol, the song distracted the snake enough to let Ranger Granger start moving slowly toward the ladder. Ebba explained to Ranger Granger that he could trust her and that the ladder was there for him to climb up. Ranger Granger was somewhat hesitant until the snake jumped at his left foot. The snake barely missed his hiking boot.

"Come on up!" yelled Daisy.
"Oh, Christmas tree! How lovely are your branches!" sang Victoria.
"You can do this, Mr. Granger. Keep climbing!" encouraged Ebba.

Ranger Granger pulled himself out of the hole, falling over Max. "Ouucchhh!" Max yelled. "Excuse you!"
Ranger Granger stood up, gathered his knapsack, and started to walk back toward his truck. All the animals sat around the hole watching the snake, but not Daisy. She had run off to Ranger Granger's truck.
"Wait! Wait! You owe Ebba a thank you, sir. She saved your life," Daisy explained.
Ebba was still sitting near the hole when Ranger Granger returned.
"Thank you, black bear. You saved my life even when you knew I wanted you put in a zoo," Ranger Granger said.
"You're welcome, sir," replied Ebba with a smile.

The animals sat and chatted until the sun began to set. Victoria even sang a new Christmas carol for the snake.

"Well, it's time for us to jet, Buttercup!" said Daisy.

"Why do you insist on calling her Buttercup? It's Ebba!" Max said, eating a woodchip.

"Because she's the sweetest bear around town," said Daisy.